Pepper
AND
Frannie

CATHERINE LAZAR ODELL

PAGE
STREET
KIDS

Pepper is practical and prepared,
and follows the rules.

Frannie is fancy and free,
and follows her own path.

Pepper and Frannie are best friends,

and they both love a good adventure.

This weekend, Pepper is planning a trip to
photograph her favorite wildflower.

Frannie is looking forward to the weekend too.

She is going to Wheels in the Woods,
her favorite skateboarding festival.

Pepper packed everything for her trip
and is right on schedule.

Frannie is not . . .

Pepper is surprised to see Frannie.

Phew! Frannie is in luck. Pepper is going the same way.

They hit the road to Wheels in the Woods.

When they arrive, Pepper is curious about the festivities.

Pepper hadn't planned to stay,
but Frannie is very convincing.

Pepper is mesmerized.

She snaps photos of perfect flips, ollies,
and tailstalls on the half pipe.

Frannie goes with the flow of the other skaters.

Then, Frannie has an idea.

Pepper hadn't planned to skate, but Frannie is very encouraging.

Pepper does not feel confident,

but Frannie is a good teacher.

She waits until Pepper is in the flow,
and then lets her go . . .

I'm doing it!

Pepper is done skating.

Frannie knows Pepper can do it,

so she convinces her to try again,

and again,

and again,

and then . . .

Frannie is stoked to skate with her best friend.
Pepper is hooked. Skateboarding is fun!

If I can do this . . .

I can do anything!

They shred, leaning into the curves and
carving down the rolling hillside, all afternoon.

Even Frannie falls sometimes . . .

and Pepper is a good friend when she does.

It was another good adventure

for Pepper and Frannie.

For my fancy friend Jesse,
and to Matthew for keeping me on course
and being there when I fall.

Copyright © 2019 Catherine Odell

First published in 2019 by Page Street Kids,
an imprint of
Page Street Publishing Co.
27 Congress Street, Suite 105
Salem, MA 01970
www.pagestreetpublishing.com

Distributed by Macmillan, sales in Canada by The Canadian Manda Group

19 20 21 22 23 CCO 5 4 3 2 1

ISBN-13: 978-1-62414-660-2
ISBN-10: 1-624-14660-0

CIP data for this book is available from the Library of Congress.

This book was typeset in Brandon Grotesque.
The illustrations were done in mixed media.

Printed and bound in Shenzhen, Guangdong, China

Page Street Publishing uses only materials from
suppliers who are committed to responsible
and sustainable forest management.

Page Street Publishing protects our planet by donating to
nonprofits like The Trustees,
which focuses on local land conservation.